The Night Before Christmas

A Brick Story

Clement C. Moore

Illustrated by
Amanda Brack

Sky Pony Press
New York

’Twas the night before Christmas, when all through the house
Not a creature was stirring, not even a mouse;

The stockings were hung by the chimney with care,
In hopes that St. Nicholas soon would be there;

The children were nestled all snug in their beds;
While visions of sugarplums danced in their heads;

And Mamma in her 'kerchief, and I in my cap,
Had just settled our brains for a long winter's nap,

When out on the lawn there arose such a clatter,
I sprang from my bed to see what was the matter.

Away to the window I flew like a flash,
Tore open the shutters and threw up the sash.

The moon on the breast of the new-fallen snow,
Gave a luster of midday to objects below,

A bundle of toys he had flung on his back,

And his clothes were all tarnished with ashes and soot;

When what to my wondering eyes did appear,
But a miniature sleigh and eight tiny reindeer,

With a little old driver so lively and quick,

I knew in a moment he must be St. Nick.

More rapid than eagles his coursers they came,
And he whistled and shouted and called them by name:
"Now, Dasher! now, Dancer! now Prancer and Vixen!
On, Comet! on, Cupid! on, Donner and Blitzen!

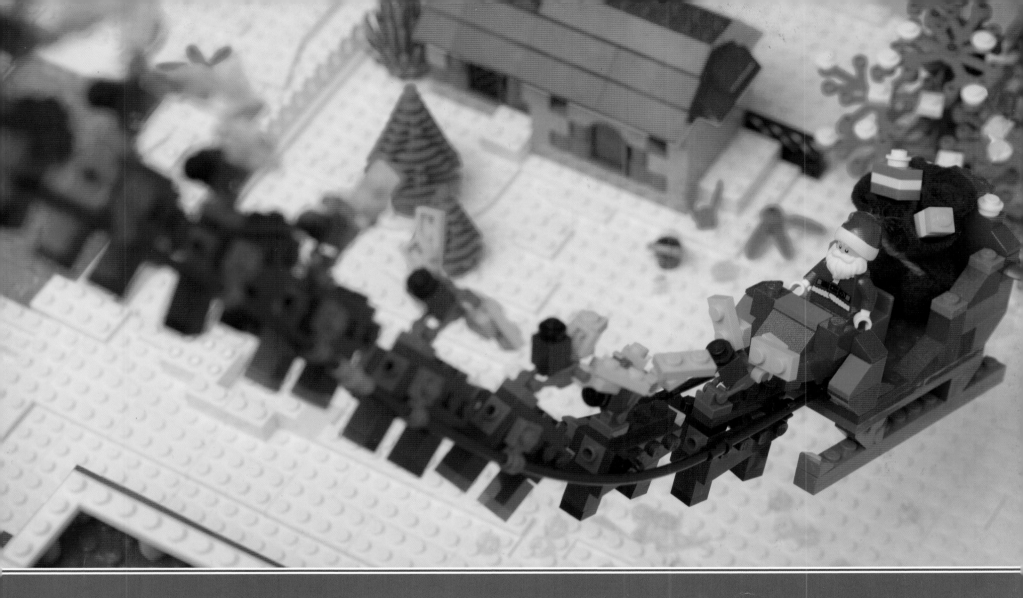

To the top of the porch! to the top of the wall!
Now dash away! dash away! dash away all!"
As leaves that before the wild hurricane fly,
When they meet with an obstacle, mount to the sky;

So up to the housetop the coursers they flew

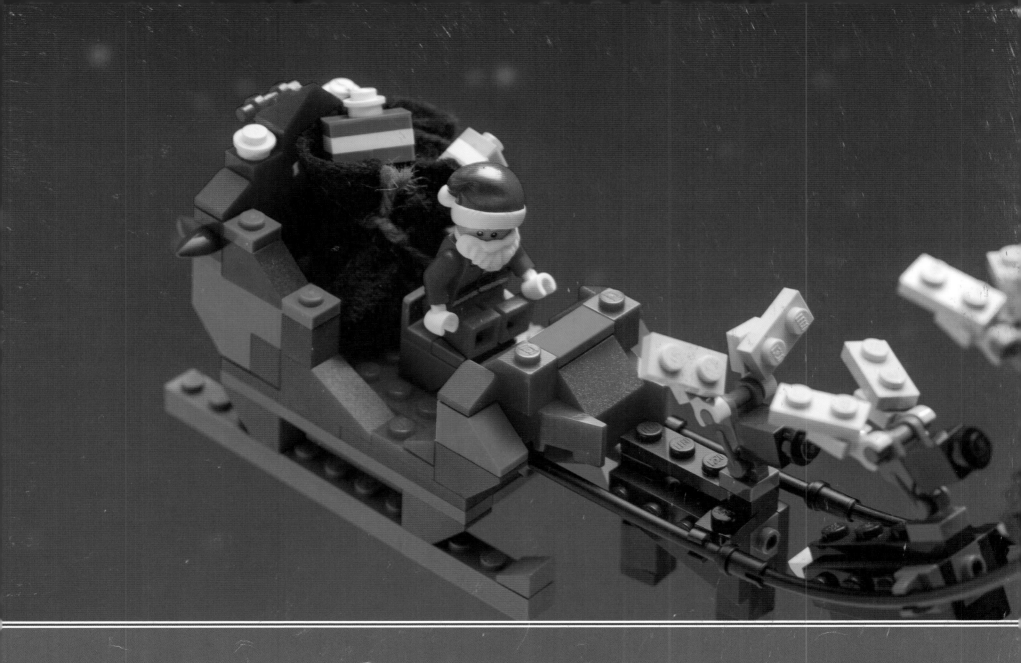

With the sleigh full of toys, and St. Nicholas, too—

And then, in a twinkling, I heard on the roof

The prancing and pawing of each little hoof.

As I drew in my head and was turning around,

Down the chimney St. Nicholas came with a bound.

He was dressed all in fur, from his head to his foot,

And he looked like a peddler just opening his pack.

His eyes—how they twinkled! His dimples, how merry!
His cheeks were like roses, his nose like a cherry!
His droll little mouth was drawn up like a bow,
And the beard on his chin was as white as the snow;

The stump of a pipe he held tight in his teeth,
And the smoke, it encircled his head like a wreath;
He had a broad face and a little round belly
That shook when he laughed, like a bowl full of jelly.

He was chubby and plump, a right jolly old elf,
And I laughed when I saw him, in spite of myself;

A wink of his eye and a twist of his head
Soon gave me to know I had nothing to dread;

He spoke not a word, but went straight to his work,
And filled all the stockings; then turned with a jerk,

And laying his finger aside of his nose,

And giving a nod, up the chimney he rose;

He sprang to his sleigh, to his team gave a whistle,
And away they all flew like the down of a thistle.

But I heard him exclaim, ere he drove out of sight:
"Happy Christmas to all, and to all a good night!"

Sky Pony Press books may be purchased in bulk at special discounts for sales promotion, corporate gifts, fund-raising, or educational purposes. Special editions can also be created to specifications. For details, contact the Special Sales Department, Sky Pony Press, 307 West 36th Street, 11th Floor, New York, NY 10018 or info@skyhorsepublishing.com.

Sky Pony® is a registered trademark of Skyhorse Publishing, Inc.®, a Delaware corporation.

Visit our website at www.skyponypress.com.

10 9 8 7 6 5 4 3 2 1

Manufactured in China, June 2015
This product conforms to CPSIA 2008

Library of Congress Cataloging-in-Publication Data

Moore, Clement Clarke, 1779-1863.
The night before Christmas : a brick story / Clement C. Moore ; illustrated by Amanda Brack.
pages cm
Summary: "Spread the Christmas cheer with this whimsical retelling of Clement C. Moore's cherished poem, "A Visit from St. Nicholas." This new edition of the classic features the text of Moore's original poem, illustrated with beautifully detailed LEGO brick scenes and characters. See the colorful stockings hung by the chimney in the fanciful brick house, and look on at the visions of dancing brick sugarplums. Turn the pages to reveal Saint Nicholas with his bundle of toys and his eight trusty reindeer, and watch as he magically slides down the chimney to bring presents to the good little girls and boys before shouting, "Now dash away, dash away, dash away all!" This treasured Christmas poem in brick will quickly become the highlight of your holiday storybooks and a great new tradition for the whole family!"-- Provided by publisher.
Summary: "Spread the Christmas cheer with this whimsical retelling of Clement C. Moore's cherished poem, "A Visit from St. Nicholas." This new edition of the classic features the text of Moore's original poem, illustrated with beautifully detailed LEGO brick scenes and characters"-- Provided by publisher.
ISBN 978-1-63450-179-8 (hardback)
1. Santa Claus--Juvenile poetry. 2. Christmas poetry. 3. Children's poetry, American. 4. LEGO toys--Juvenile literature. I. Brack, Amanda, illustrator. II. Title.
PS2429.M5N5 2015c
811'.2--dc23
2015011264

Cover design by Sarah Brody
Cover photo credit Amanda Brack

Ebook ISBN: 978-1-63450-922-0